HOW TO

READ

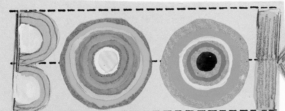

A BOOK

BY

KWAME
ALEXANDER

Art by
MELISSA
SWEET

HARPER An Imprint of HarperCollins Publishers

For Samayah
—K.A.

For Dana
—M.S.

FIRST, FIND A TREE—
BLACK TUPELO OR
DAWN REDWOOD WILL DO—
AND PLANT YOURSELF.

(IT'S OKAY IF YOU PREFER A STOOP, LIKE LANGSTON HUGHES.)

ONCE YOU'RE COMFY, PEEL ITS GENTLE SKIN, LIKE YOU WOULD A CLEMENTINE

THE COLOR OF

SUNRISE

SUNRISE

LONGMANS

"Look, look, Mother!" Bambi e
"There's a flower flying."
"That's not a flower," said his mothe
butterfly."
Bambi stared at the butterfly, en
ha tly from a blade of
its giddy way.
tterfl

NEXT,

DIG YOUR THUMB
AT THE BOTTOM
OF EACH JUICY SECTION
AND

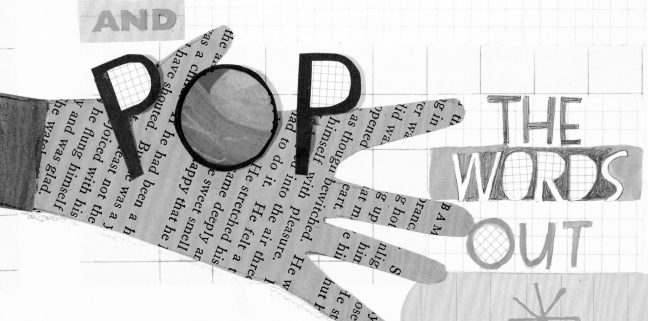

POP
THE
WORDS
OUT

*

PAGE BY RUSTLING PAGE.

THEN, WHEN THE SUN IS SO QUIET, WATCH A NOVEL WORLD UNFURL RIGHT BEFORE YOUR EYES-------✳

SURPRISE!

it's a BOOK PARTY

STACKED WITH ALL
YOUR FAVORITE
FRIENDS:
A PICNIC OF
WORDS + SOUNDS
IN LEAPS + BOUNDS.

SO GET
REAL COZY
BETWEEN
THE COVERS
AND LET YOUR
FINGERS WONDER

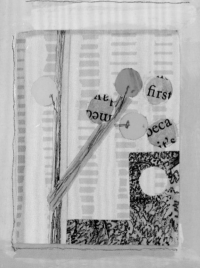

AS THEY WANDER...

SQUEEZE EVERY MORSEL OF EACH PLUMP LINE UNTIL THE LAST DROP OF MAGIC

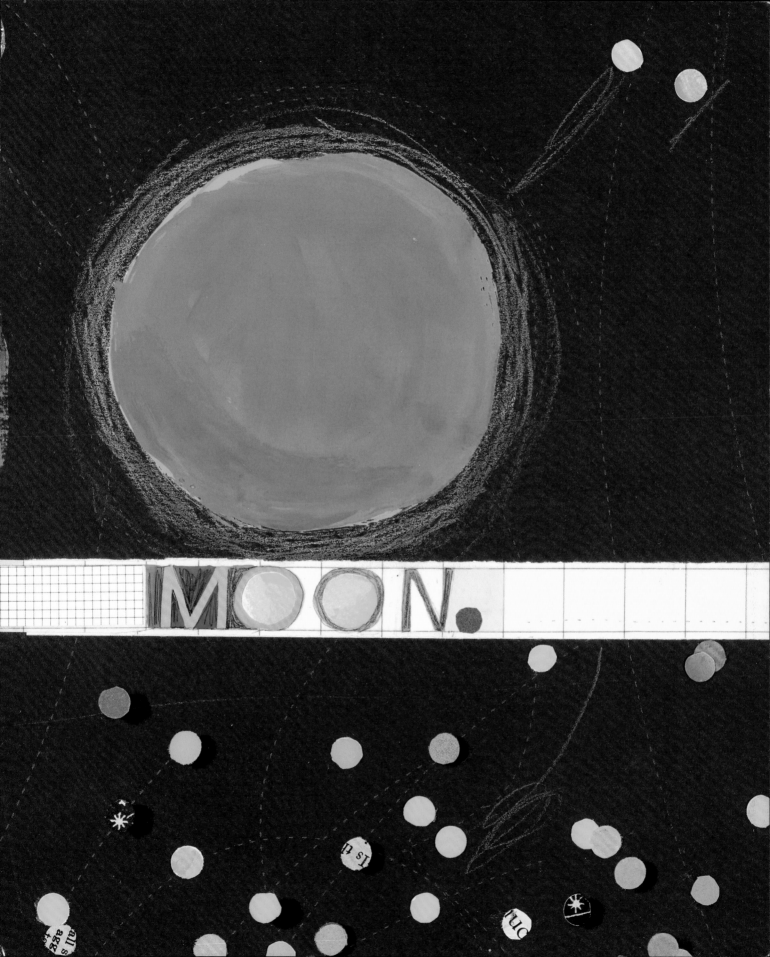

MOON.

DON'T RUSH THOUGH:

YOUR EYES NEED

TIME TO TASTE.

YOUR SOUL NEEDS

ROOM TO BLOOM.

NOW, SLEEP.
DREAM.
HOPE.
(YOU NEVER REACH)

A Note from Kwame Alexander

I wrote this poem for World Read Aloud Day in 2010. My friend Pam Allyn, founder of the global literacy organization LitWorld, commissioned me to write a poem about the joy and power of reading. In my excitement, I wrote three for her to consider. "How to Read a Book" was one of the three, and it was, by far, my absolute favorite. But she didn't choose it. In all fairness, the one she selected was pretty cool too. It had a clever metaphor about finding inspiration on the corner "Where the Sidewalk Ends" (see what I did there?).

I'm not sure where the idea for "How to Read a Book" came from. Maybe I was eating a clementine. Or reading Langston Hughes and Shel Silverstein. My daughter was two at the time, so it's very likely I was spending a lot of time in our local park, under a tree, on a blanket, doing both.

Every parent knows there is always that one book that the kid wants to hear over and over again. For mine, it was *Miffy*. We read it in the mornings, at naptime, in the car, and at bedtime. She simply never wanted it to end, and each time, she smiled and laughed and wriggled and *ahhh*ed, like it was always the first time. I think writing the poem that became this book was my way of capturing our family reading experience on paper. Of painting a picture of the journey readers take each time they crack open a book, get lost in the pages, and wander through the wonder.

A few months after I archived it, Loudoun County Public Library in Virginia asked if I had a poem to celebrate reading that they could put on a poster for National Poetry Month. I'd learned my lesson, so I only gave them one poem. They loved it. I hope you do too.

A Note from Melissa Sweet

When I first read Kwame's poem, it put into words how captivating it can feel to read a book. As the illustrator and a collage artist, I wondered: What kind of images would best reflect Kwame's words?

My collages often include pages from discarded books, tattered book covers, along with paint and other materials (in this book there's also a paint can lid and bits of wood).

After trying all sorts of materials, I began using the pages from a worn-out copy of *Bambi* within the collages. I chose it because I loved the imagery of the fawn, the paper was a beautiful color, and because it was once a beloved children's book.

Then one day, well into making the art, I read a poem by Nikki Giovanni that began:

poetry is motion graceful

as a fawn

That was the perfect affirmation. The serendipity of using *Bambi* as part of the art made me trust the imagery was heading in the right direction.

Nikki's poem also inspired the three-dimensional collage incorporating her words at the beginning of the book, setting the stage for Kwame's lyrical text.

Finally, I began painting with neon colors, not just to convey how exhilarating and electrifying it can feel to read a book but, as Kwame writes, to find "the last drop of magic."

I'm grateful to Kwame, and to everyone at HarperCollins, for making this book all that I dreamed it could be. I hope you never reach the end.